Thomas Durfee

Some Thoughts on the Constitution of Rhode Island

Thomas Durfee

Some Thoughts on the Constitution of Rhode Island

ISBN/EAN: 9783337380656

Printed in Europe, USA, Canada, Australia, Japan

Cover: Foto ©Andreas Hilbeck / pixelio.de

More available books at **www.hansebooks.com**

SOME THOUGHTS

ON THE

CONSTITUTION OF RHODE ISLAND.

.

BY

THOMAS DURFEE.

———◆———

PROVIDENCE
SIDNEY S. RIDER.
1884.

PRINTED BY THE PROVIDENCE PRESS COMPANY.

THOUGHTS ON THE CONSTITUTION

OF RHODE ISLAND.

It is now more than forty years since the Constitution of
the State was adopted. Those forty years have been years
of extraordinary progress. In 1840, the population of the
State was 108,830. In 1880, the population was 276,710,
an increase of over one hundred and fifty per cent. I have
not the figures in regard to the wealth of the State in 1840,
but in 1850, ten years later, the true wealth was estimated
at $80,508,794. In 1880, the estimate was $400,000,000.
No other New England State has increased so rapidly in
either population or wealth. No other State of the Union
has so much wealth according to its population or so large a
population according to its size. The proofs of this progress are patent to observation, in the growth of cities and
villages; in the increase of mills, factories and shops; in
market, and mart, and thoroughfare; in improved modes
and means of transport and inter-communication; in places
and appliances for recreation and enjoyment; in the multi-
plication of happy homes and magnificent mansions. The
progress is not limited to special classes or pursuits; but
the poor share in it with the rich, the country with the city.
Pauperism has been reduced to a minimum. The savings
banks show a deposit of $50,127,806.08. Every sort of
productive labor is fairly, if not richly, remunerated. What
other State is there in which there is a higher average of human happiness? Let the defamers of Rhode Island tell us.
Of course, there may be particular men, or particular classes

of men, who can find elsewhere more to delight or instruct them ; but what I mean to ask is, not where can the artist or the scholar or the man of affluence and leisure pass his life with the greatest profit or pleasure, but where, taking men in the mass and striking an average, is there a happier people than the people of Rhode Island? I repeat, let our defamers answer the question. Meanwhile, the fact that it can be seriously asked, is in itself a practical refutation of their slanders ; for most certainly a State that has so greatly prospered cannot have been badly governed.

Progress in Rhode Island has not been merely a material progress. Education has been a matter of public concern. Schools abound, and excellent teachers, paid from the public purse, are everywhere supplied. The people have become a people of readers. Free libraries, encouraged and endowed by the State, spring up in village and hamlet to satisfy the popular thirst for knowledge. Illiteracy exists, without doubt ; but if any Rhode Islander has grown up illiterate during the last forty years, the State is surely not to blame for it. I confess, I do not anticipate the great results which some anticipate from a general addiction to indiscriminate reading. Knowledge, especially the knowledge gathered from books and newspapers, is not power until applied to use, nor wisdom until converted into character. Knowledge, however, merely as knowledge, is a good, unless abused, and in Rhode Island the doors of knowledge are open to all.

There is something more indispensable to the public welfare than either wealth or education, namely, virtue. The imperishable foundation of every permanent polity is righteousness. I do not care to claim for Rhode Island any preeminence in this respect. I am too profoundly sensible how infinitely she falls below what she ought to be, to do it ; but nevertheless, I venture to think that nowhere else are life and property safer or crime less prevalent. The law is efficacious without cruelty, endeavoring to reform as well as to punish the offender. A liberal charity, constantly multiplying its institutions and agencies, ministers to the needs of the suffering and the destitute. Nowhere do men of all ranks and conditions associate on kindlier terms. The State, faithful to her fundamental principle, is hospitable to every legitimate form of freedom in thought or speech. The most aggressive thinker can get hearers, even when he gains no disciples. There is no surer test of magnanimity than this. Sometimes one is led to fear that a plethora of riches, pampering the senses with luxury and the mind with delicate delights, may destroy the manlier virtues without which prosperity is a delusion. Doubtless the danger threatens and ought to be counteracted by every sort of virile exercise and discipline. But fortunately, as yet, it only threatens; for we all know, and are all proud to know, that, in the recent war for the Union, as well as in the earlier war for independence, the men of Rhode Island were still conspicuous, among the bravest of their comrades, for the heroic courage, the fortitude, the patriotism and the generous self-devotion with which they everywhere acquitted themselves.

"The tree is known by its fruits." Judged by this criterion, approved alike by inspired wisdom and practical experience, the State has no reason to fear comparison with her sisters. But there are those who reject this criterion. They hold that a tree may bring forth good fruit and yet be a bad tree, if it differs from what they think it ought to be, and so they condemn it, as fit only to be up-rooted and destroyed. They think the prosperity of the State is no proof that its government is good. They dislike the constitution because it does not correspond with their conception of what it ought to be, and therefore, regardless of the benefits which have accrued from it, and of the political customs and habitudes of the people, they denounce it as an instrument of iniquity, and disparage its authors, the fathers whom we have been taught to venerate, as men of narrow mind and illiberal spirit. They prefer theory and sentiment to prac-

tical policy and experience. They hate the constitution because their feelings have been exasperated against it. But
if feeling is to be the criterion, there is feeling for the constitution and its authors as well as against them. Indeed,
it sorely tries the feelings of some of us, who are not too
young to remember what sort of men they were, the mak-
ers of the constitution, now so flippantly maligned, and who
are not too dull of discernment to see what sort of men they
are who presume to malign them,—it tries our feelings, I
say, when we hear those many respectable citizens, the intelligent legislators, learned lawyers and sagacious statesmen of a
former generation, all of them enlightened lovers of the State,
Rhode Islanders to the marrow, so wantonly contemned and
calumniated in their graves. But this is sentiment. It no
more follows that the constitution is good because some
of us have learned to respect and revere its authors, than
that it is bad because others have learned to despise and re-
vile them. It is good or bad, not according as the men who
made it were good or bad, but according as it works well or
ill; though most assuredly it behooves us, if its authors were
wise and patriotic men, not to condemn it until we have first
ascertained and carefully considered the reasons which led
them to make it as they did, and until, enlightened by this
study as well as by our own experience, we are satisfied that
their work, however well intended, has, in its practical operation, turned out to be a failure.

The constitution was not, as it has been ignorantly called,
a mere partisan instrument. It was the crowning work of
the Law and Order party,—a party containing some of the
best elements of both the great parties of the day. Demo-
crats like James Fenner, John Brown Francis, Elisha R.
Potter, Richard W. Greene, and Francis Wayland, were as
prominent in the party as Whigs like John Whipple, James
F. Simmons, Samuel Ames, William G. Goddard, Henry B.
Anthony and Thomas A. Jenckes. A person can have no
excuse for speaking of these men as narrow-minded, except

that he speaks rashly, without knowing them. They ardently loved the State, and if they put peculiar provisions in the constitution, we may be sure that they put them there, not because they were political bigots or aristocrats, but because they thought the good of the State demanded them. And, therefore, again remarking that the constitution, because made or adopted by such men, deserves to be studied before it is condemned, I wish to inquire into the reasonableness of some of its provisions which have been violently attacked.

The principal objection brought against the constitution is, that the naturalized citizen has no right to vote under it unless he is the owner of a freehold estate in land of the clear total value of one hundred and thirty-four dollars, or, of the clear annual rental value of seven dollars; whereas the native citizen, otherwise qualified, is permitted to vote on the payment of a tax of one dollar, assessed on his real or personal property or on him personally as a registry voter. This discrimination between the native and the naturalized citizen is denounced as invidious, impolitic and unjust. The discrimination originated, not in any curtailment by the constitution of the right of suffrage, but in an extension of it; the extension being conceded only in favor of the native citizen. We are, therefore, to inquire why it was that our fathers, when they extended the right of suffrage, did not extend it to all the citizens alike, and, having ascertained why they discriminated between the native and the naturalized, to consider whether, in the light of their reasons for it, the discrimination is to be regarded as invidious, impolitic and unjust.

I was but a boy when the constitution was adopted; but the time was full of interest for boys as well as men, and I remember what was said. If Rhode Island had been simply an agricultural state, like Vermont or New Hampshire, I think there would have been no discrimination. The immigrants into such states are not numerous, and, scattering abroad, they quickly identify themselves with the native population, ceasing to be a distinct element. They thus became assimilated to the native citizens in interest, feeling and opinion, and may be safely trusted with an equal right of suffrage. If Rhode Island had been a large State, like Massachusetts, possibly she might, though a manufacturing State, have foregone any discrimination, trusting to her numerous native population to ballast the body politic and insure stability. But Rhode Island was both a small and a manufacturing State, and therefore she considered it a matter of prudent policy to give a larger right of suffrage to her native than to her naturalized citizens. Our fathers argued in this wise, that the State being small, the native population would be small, and that the rapidly increasing number of citizens of foreign birth, congregating in villages and acting together, would, with an equal right of suffrage, hold the balance of power and might easily wield a controlling influence. They were unwilling, however democratically inclined, to surrender the State into the hands of men, born and bred abroad, and therefore unfamiliar with our institutions.

Our fathers further argued that a manufacturing population — for Rhode Island had already become a distinctively manufacturing State — is likely to be not only a foreign-born but also a floating population. The operatives of mills and factories, yielding to the fluctuations of business, or to the migratory moods of their own minds, come and go continually and do not plant themselves in permanent homes. They do not take root and grow, if I may use the figure, in the social and political soil and air of Rhode Island until they become in fact, as well as in legal form, naturalized Rhode Islanders. They do not acquaint themselves with the people, the history, the institutions and the laws of the State. They are, therefore, easily manipulated and misled in politics by men who, electioneering for themselves or others, do not scruple to play upon their prejudices and passions for personal or party ends. They are too prone to move in masses without the regulative sense or sentiment of individual duty. Now our fathers saw all this, and they saw it more clearly, perhaps, than we see it, for they had been led by the political upheaval of the time to study the entire volume, not only of political principles, but also of political practices, from end to end, and, after reasoning together, they concluded that the best safeguard against this particular danger was still to hold on to the old freehold qualification for the foreign-born elector. They were doubtless led to this conclusion not only by their past experience, but also by a sort of prophetic instinct; for they clearly foresaw that the ownership of Rhode Island soil would give an almost infallible assurance that the owner intended to adopt Rhode Island as his permanent home, and, as a general rule, to become the founder of a new Rhode Island family, thus giving the best possible pledges of his attachment to the State and of his interest in its well-being. The forty years of unexampled prosperity which have since ensued, bear witness to the wisdom of their conclusion.

Now, having set forth the reasons for the discrimination, let us consider whether the reasons are valid. There are some who argue that the right of suffrage is incident to citizenship, and therefore cannot be lawfully denied to any citizen. This is an error. A voter is almost always a citizen, but a citizen is not necessarily a voter. Women and children are citizens, but they are not voters. Others argue, still more erroneously, that the right of suffrage is a natural right, belonging to every man by virtue of his manhood as soon as he comes of age, and therefore cannot be withheld from him without committing a gross wrong. It is useless to reason with men who maintain this doctrine, for they are generally men whose minds are be-mired in a metaphysical muddle. The right to vote is not a natural, but a political right. It cannot exist in a state of nature, if there ever be such a state. It cannot exist until men unite in

2

some form of political organization, and then it depends, for its existence and character, on the rule which they adopt, or which gradually grows up among them, as their fundamental law or constitution. I shall therefore assume, without any further discussion of these points, that there is no right of suffrage other than that which the constitution confers.

It is sometimes said that, considering men merely as men, one has as much right as another to have his will prevail, and that, therefore, anything short of an equal right of suffrage, whatever the law may ordain, is unjust. This is a point which merits a moment's attention. The argument involves a subtle fallacy or self-contradiction; for man merely as man, has no right, *i. e.*, no political right. A man merely as man is simply an isolated individual. He may have a right to assert his will *against* others for his own protection, but not *over* others to bring them into subjection. What do we mean by "right"—not moral, but civil or political right? Right cannot exist in one man independently of duty in another or others. If A has a right to have his will prevail over B, by voting, it is because it is the duty of B to submit to the will of A, so signified. If a majority has a right to have its will prevail over a minority, by voting, it is because it is the duty of the minority to submit to the will of the majority, so signified. But what is it which creates this duty? I know of nothing which creates it but the law. Without the law, might is right, and weakness is duty; or, in other words, without law, there is no such thing as right, in the sense in which we are using the word. The very conception of right, therefore, introduces us into the sphere of law; that is to say, into a sphere in which the mere relation of man to man is subject to the higher relation of man to society, organized as the State. In that sphere we can no longer consider man merely as man,—the attempt to do so is confusing and anarchical—but we are bound to consider him as an integer of the State, and, inasmuch as the State is more important than any individual in it, the question of

what is best for the State, takes precedence of what is best
for the individual. It may be said that what is best for the
State, is, in the long run, what is best for the individual. I
do not dispute it. But, conceding that the two questions
are identical, nevertheless, to consider what is best for the
State, in preference to what is best for the individual, is to
consider the question from the higher, because more com-
prehensive, point of view. I shall, therefore, adopt this
higher point of view, and inquire, not whether this or that
naturalized citizen, considering him simply as a man, has as
just a claim to vote as this or that native citizen, considering
him simply as a man; but whether, taking Rhode Island as
it is to-day, it is best for the State as a whole to let the naturalized vote as freely as the native citizen. In other words,
I propose to look at a purely political question from a political point of view.

It is sometimes argued that it is bad for a State to have
any considerable number of disaffected citizens in it; and,
it is said, the naturalized citizens of Rhode Island are disaffected because they feel that they are unfairly treated.
Doubtless disaffection is an evil, but if the remedy be worse
than the evil, it is better to bear than to cure it. I think,
however, that the disaffection is overrated. A few tonguey
men can do a deal of talking and easily create an impression
which grossly exaggerates the reality. Indeed, when you
come to the business of talking, there is nobody who can do
so much of it on so small a capital of thinking as the fault-
finder. The great majority of our naturalized citizens are
satisfied with their political status — they are too sensible to
be dissatisfied. The peculiarity of our constitution is notorious. It has been bruited abroad to the four corners of the
world. There is probably not a naturalized citizen in Rhode
Island, who has any interest in politics, who did not know,
when he came to the State, that he could not vote here without a freehold qualification. If he came knowing this, he

12

came assenting to it ; and why should he quarrel with a condition which he voluntarily accepted? As a rule, he does not quarrel with it, but some self-constituted champion of his cause quarrels with it for him. Some of the wisest of our citizens of foreign birth not only do not complain, but they applaud; for they see that the discrimination is not only a prudent political safeguard, but likewise that it has exerted a salutary influence over their fellow-countrymen, in that it has been an incentive to industry and frugality, so that many of them, who would else have been penniless, are the owners of happy homes and the fathers of thriving families. Of course, when I say this, I do not ignore the fact that there are naturalized citizens in Rhode Island, discontented with their political lot, who loudly and even angrily proclaim it. Some men are easily soured to the point of fermentation. They cannot see others enjoying privileges which are denied to them without resentment. This is human nature. There are good men among these whom we would all be glad to know as voters, especially if they would cultivate a sweeter temper. But we cannot abolish a good law because it works unpleasantly in individual cases. The most clamorous complaint, however, does not come from these men. It comes rather from ambitious politicians, who are not personally affected by the discrimination, but who think their following is lessened by it. They certainly cannot claim to have the discrimination abolished, unless they can show that it is detrimental to the State as well as to themselves.

There are men who object to the freehold qualification because it is a property qualification, and who contend that an educational one would be better. Their argument is, that a man who owns real estate is no better qualified to vote than if he did not own it, whereas intelligence is a real qualification. The argument is, in my opinion, rather specious than sound. Generally the men who acquire real estate will be the better educated of their class, even if we have regard only to education by school or book, which is what these re-

formers mean by education. But men who have had any
considerable experience of life, know that a mere superficial
book or school education, which is all that could be required
as a qualification for voting, is not the best. The laborer,
who, coming here from a foreign country, labors steadily
and lays by a percentage of his wages, month by month and
year by year, until out of the accumulation of his small savings he buys a lot of land, builds a house, and, establishing
himself in it, rears his children to better advantages than
his own, will have educated himself with an education which
will be much surer to improve him and make him valuable
as a citizen and a voter than any which he would have been
likely to acquire from book or school. He will have acquired habits of industry, self-denial, thrift and forethought.
He will also have acquired a sturdy independence of character,
which will go far to protect him against the wiles of unscru-
pulous demagogues. It is absurd to say that such a man is
uneducated because he is illiterate. Moreover, by becom-
ing an owner of Rhode Island soil, he will have identified
himself with the State, and will be sure to feel — such is human nature — a stronger and steadier interest in its welfare.

There is a matter connected with the extension of the
right of suffrage which has never yet attracted the attention
which it deserves. Under our law, all persons who are qualified to vote upon any proposition to impose a tax, or for the
expenditure of money in any town, are liable to serve as jurors, unless specially exempted. It is safe to assume that,
so long as the right of jury trial exists, this liability will not
be restricted. To extend the right of suffrage as proposed
will add largely to the number of those who are liable to
jury duty. Will it not add largely to the growing distrust
of jury trials? I am not one of those who wish to see trial
by jury abolished. I know of no better mode of trial for
questions of fact than trial by jury, if the jurors be com-
petent. Nothing would have been more shocking to our
revolutionary ancestors than the thought of abolishing it;

for they regarded it as a great popular right, trial by jury
being the mode in which the people participate in judicial
proceedings. It is clear to me, however, that it is gradually
losing favor. There are two reasons for this. One is, that
our modern methods of business develop many questions of
mixed law and fact which require careful study and attention, with more than an average degree of analytical acu-
men, to decide them correctly. The other is, that the ordi-
nary *personnel* of the jury has deteriorated. To retrieve
the reputation of trial by jury, we must have better jurors.
To make good jurors, men must be not only intelligent, but
educated to a nice sense of personal responsibility. An extension of the right of suffrage to a multitude of men of
foreign birth, many of them without any capacity for pro-
tracted and discriminating attention, does not promise much
for the improvement of our jury system. In other States,
where the right of suffrage is unlimited, trial by jury has so
utterly fallen into disrepute that it has been largely super-
ceded by trial by referees.

We often hear the electoral law of the State objected to
because it differs from the electoral laws of other States.
The objection seems to have great weight with many minds,
but I profess an utter inability to appreciate it. Rhode
Island has always, for the last two hundred and fifty years,
asserted the right to think for herself. I do not believe that
any genuine Rhode Islander, who pauses a moment to re-
flect, will decide that the time has come for her to renounce
that right. The great statesmen of other lands, who have
studied our system of national and state government, have
admired it chiefly because it gives room for the free and diversified development of many different communities, at the
same time that it masses and consolidates the irresistible
strength of the entire people. These reformers, who are so
enamored of uniformity of legislation that they would gladly
remove everything that distinguishes one State from another
but its boundary lines, have only to accomplish their aim,

and the boundary lines will likewise speedily vanish, leaving nothing but a dead level of democratic, probably culminating at last in autocratic, absolutism.

We come back, therefore, to the true question, namely, will it be for the benefit of the State to have the elective franchise given as freely to our citizens of foreign birth as to our native citizens? There are men who think they make a strong point when they tell us that it is ungenerous to refuse to others the privileges which we enjoy ourselves. The elective franchise is more than a privilege, it is a power. It is sometimes said to be a trust; it is a trust,—a power held in trust, the electors being the trustees. It is our duty, therefore, to inquire, not whether it be generous, but whether it be wise, judicious, prudent, to entrust this power, so vital to the State, without restriction to our naturalized citizens. I admit again that our naturalized citizens include men of high character and intelligence, and many worthy and honest men, less intelligent, but loyal and true, whom I would willingly see registered among our voters. The fact that our naturalized citizens include such men, gives strength to the pressure for an extension of the suffrage. But these men do not constitute the main body of our foreign-born population. The main body have only the crudest political ideas. They have but little time and no good opportunities to improve themselves. How can they discharge an electoral trust in a proper manner? They cannot. They are necessarily more or less at the mercy of men who are ready to mislead or corrupt them.

I do not deceive myself. I know that what I say is not a popular thing to say. In the old world there is a sort of men who frequent the courts of kings. Their chief study is how to gain the royal favor. They avoid the utterance of all disagreeable truths. They accustom themselves to the language of unmeaning compliment. They live in an atmosphere of insincerity until the bracing and wholesome air of veracity is offensive to them. They are flatterers of kings — courtiers. In this country the court is paid to the people. The courtiers practice how to say most adroitly what is pleasing to the popular ear. Consequently they deal in captivating catch-words. They call unlimited suffrage "manhood suffrage" and resent any objection to it as if it were an objection to manhood. Or else they call it "equal rights," and resent any objection to it as if it were an arrogant assertion of superiority. They thus flatter the popular pride or appeal to the popular prejudice. Now I confess to some little distrust of these empty phrases, these barren abstractions, hollow masks of thought, which look so solid and are so specious. Let us free our minds of cant, and look the living facts in the face. Any one of my readers who, after casting his vote on election day, has lingered a few moments in the voting-room, has doubtless seen men coming in by couples, from time to time, one apparently conducting the other, handing him his ballot, marching him to the polls, and, only after the ballot has been deposited, allowing him to depart. Not unfrequently the person so brought in is more or less intoxicated. Sometimes he wears the surly hang-dog look of a voter who has made merchandise of his vote. Again and again the scene is repeated. What does it mean? It means that the "fuglemen,"—the "bosses"— of the one party or the other, or of both, are accomplishing their election jobs, and that these pliant or corrupt voters — tools in their hands — instead of voting, are "being voted." The astonished spectator, after witnessing the spectacle awhile, begins to get a glimmering notion of the difference between "manhood suffrage" as a captivating theory and "manhood suffrage" as it too often exists in matter of fact.

A free extension of the suffrage to our foreign-born citizens will surely add largely to the class of voters who, instead of voting, "are voted." And what does that signify? It signifies a reign of "the bosses." Your Boss Tweed or Boss Kelly is only the big toad in the puddle. This is not

imagination. It is fact as it exists to-day in New York, in
Boston, and in other large cities. There can be but little
doubt that it will be fact in Providence and in other Rhode
Island towns, where there are manufacturing villages, if
the suffrage be extended. It will be said, perhaps, that a
reign of the manufacturers is more probable than a reign
of the "bosses." The distinction, to my mind, is immate-
rial. The manufacturer himself is but a stronger "boss,"
when he stoops to manipulate his men. We have had
that kind of manufacturers. I do not want to see the kind
perpetuated, especially if their domination is to be intensified by unlimited suffrage.

But if such a reign ensues, what will follow? This will
follow: the bosses will become the distributors of political office and they will either take the offices themselves
or give them to their favorites; their favorites being the
men who truckle and defer to them. Have we not been wit-
nesses to this result in other States? The evil will be intensified in Rhode Island, as Rhode Island is smaller and
more densely populated. Moreover, it will be intensified,
as the foreign-born are relatively more numerous in Rhode
Island than in any but a few of the new States of the far
west, and, together with those whose parents were foreign-
born, constitute more than half the population. Corruption
will follow. Public men who serve the State from purely
disinterested motives, because the service is their natural
calling, will do so no longer. They will find it impossible
to do so without deferring to these petty despots, and such
deference is inconsistent with disinterestedness. It has been
a great benefit to the State that there have always hitherto
been men in the General Assembly who, coming there
year after year, have applied their legislative experience and
large knowledge of affairs to the maintenance of a safe and
judicious course of legislation. Benjamin Hazard, Elisha
R. Potter, both father and son, Wilkins Updike, Henry Y.
Cranston, Nathan F. Dixon and William P. Sheffield are a

3

few of many examples. It will be a public calamity when this
class of men, recoiling from a sacrifice of their self-respect,
retire from the service of the State. The cry of the day is for
"administrative reform"; but, in my humble opinion, Rhode
Island, with her complex and diversified development, has
more to fear from crude and empirical legislation, or from
mischievous over-legislation, than from bad administration;
and, with unlimited suffrage to inflame the competition for
votes, the danger of such legislation and over-legislation
will be indefinitely increased.

I will not detain the reader longer on this point. Much
more might be said, and much more will doubtless occur to
the reader himself. I have shown the reasons why our fathers
bestowed the suffrage less liberally on naturalized than on
native citizens. I have endeavored to show that these reasons were at first, and still continue to be valid. A word
more in conclusion. If any naturalized citizen be really in
earnest in his desire to vote, he can easily qualify himself.
If he chooses not to qualify, he may nevertheless have the
satisfaction of knowing that his sons, born in the United
States, are native citizens, and that as such they can vote as
soon as they are of age. He may also have the satisfaction
of knowing that, though he cannot vote himself, there are
many native and many naturalized citizens, whose interests
are similar to his, whatever his may be, who, when they
vote, will vote for him as well as for themselves, so that,
though voteless, he will not be unrepresented.

The second objection to the constitution is, that the representation is unequal in the General Assembly under it.
Under it the senate consists of the Lieutenant-Governor and
of one senator from each town or city in the State, and the
house of representatives of seventy-two members, appor-
tioned among the towns according to their population, except that every town is entitled to at least one member, and
no town or city to more than twelve. The result is, that on
a call of the senate, the city of Providence counts no more

than the little town of Jamestown, and, on a call of the house, can never count more than one-sixth of the entire body, though it already has nearly two-fifths of the population of the State. The complaint is, that this is on the face of it indefensible. I have no doubt that Providence has increased, relatively to other towns, more rapidly than was anticipated when the constitution was adopted. I do not think it would be unreasonable for her to have a little larger representation, though personally I do not care for it. The enemies of our constitution, however, are not satisfied with a simple increase : they demand an utter subversion of the basis of representation. They demand that the State shall be divided into districts of equal population, and shall be represented in the senate by one senator from each district, and that the several towns and cities shall be represented in the lower house according to population. Any other rule, they say, is unequal, and consequently unjust. But if they think equality is so great a desideratum, it seems to me that, in order to be consistent, they ought to go a step further and prescribe a standard of legislative capacity, and disallow any representative having the capacity in any greater or less degree ; for it occasionally happens that a town with only one representative is more effectively represented than some more populous town with half a dozen. The city of Providence, with its hundred and twenty thousand inhabitants to pick and choose from, has manifestly very great advantages in this respect.

But let us treat the matter seriously and try it by our test question ; that is, will the State at large be the better for such an equal representation? I cannot profess to give from memory the reasons which prevailed with our fathers in prescribing the rule of representation, for I do not remember to have heard them discussed. It is apparent, however, that they deferred to a dominant town feeling. Such a feeling is hereditary in Rhode Island. It is rooted in the history of the State. The first towns were separate commonwealths, and,

even after their union under the charter, they continued to
exercise large local powers. It was, therefore, natural for
our fathers to treat them with consideration. They treated
them as in some sort distinct political entities, giving each a
senator, and each a representative, increasing the representatives according to population up to the limit of twelve.
Evidently they were not so infatuated with the doctrine of
equality as to be willing to sacrifice to it the individual
character of the State. Evidently they perceived, what our
modern constitution-mongers seem to be incapable of per-
ceiving, that a *State*, particularly a State which has ex-
isted for more than two centuries, is what the word imports,
something that *stays* or *stands*, and not a mere diagram on a
blackboard, which can be rubbed out and reconstructed, *ad
libitum*, with a wet sponge and a piece of chalk. Moreover,
it is evident that, in this as in other respects, our fathers
took the constitution of the United States as a pattern to
go by. Under our constitution the towns have very nearly
the relation to each other which the States have to each
other under the constitution of the United States. It was
thus that, haply building better than they knew, they paid
instinctive homage to the great instrument under which little
Rhode Island is co-equal with mighty New York or Texas in
the federal senate. They did not promulgate any doctrine
which would discredit her among her sisters. But these in-
dustrious disseminators of the new creed, that unequal representation is legalized iniquity,—how can they defend the
federal status of Rhode Island without the most egregious
self-stultification?

The doctrine that an unequal representation is necessarily
iniquitous is predicated mainly on the idea that the representative is simply the delegate or mouth-piece of his constituency. There is doubtless a modicum of truth in this
idea, inasmuch as every representative stands nearer to his
own than to any other constituency; but there is only
truth enough in it to make it dangerous; for unques-

tionably the *first* duty of every representative is to the State, and he has no right to prefer the interest of his constituency to the interest of the State. The legislator who has not risen to this conception of his duty, has yet to learn the first great lesson of legislation. Now there is nothing which is better calculated to teach this lesson, unobtrusively but effectually, than this very inequality of representation; for certainly the senator from Jamestown, when he sees that he counts as much as the senator from Providence, cannot think that he was endowed with this parity of power simply for the sake of Jamestown, or for any other reason than because it was intended that he and the senator from Providence should both alike yield a ready obedience to the same paramount duty, namely, the duty of serving the State always to the best of their abilities; and the senator from Providence, when he sees that, notwithstanding the manifold interests of the city, he counts for no more than the senator from the smallest town, cannot think that he was thus slenderly endowed out of enmity to the city or for any other reason than because he has a right to appeal with confidence to every one of his fellow-senators for assistance in the accomplishment of whatever is for the common benefit of the city and the State, and likewise even of whatever is for the particular benefit of the city, if it be consistent with the general good. I do not wish to press the point unduly, but I venture to ask any one who has had experience, if what I have been saying is not exactly according to the fact. It is notorious that the senator from Providence wields an extraordinary power, cheerfully conceded, not to him personally, but to his representative position, and that it seldom or never happens that the city can truly complain that she has suffered from either prejudice or envy or ill-will on the part of the country towns. Who that had the good fortune to see the late John Brown Francis occupying his senatorial seat, year after year, with never-failing courtesy and wisdom, ever had any other thought than that, though elected by Warwick, he sat there for Rhode Island? Or, again, who that watched the long and eminently unselfish career of the late Nathan F. Dixon, ever thought of regarding him simply as the member from Westerly, or ever felt that the other towns of the State owed the town of Westerly anything but gratitude for electing him so uninterruptedly, and thus affording them the benefit of his extraordinary good sense and long legislative experience? I mention these men, not because they were exceptional, but because they are typical of a large class of useful legislators, trained to the public service under our system of representation. Would the State be better served if the representation were equalized according to the plan of our so-called reformers? Let the reader pause and ponder before he answers the question.

The plan is professedly urged chiefly for the benefit of the city of Providence, because the inequality is the more glaring in the case of the city. Our reformers, however, are very careful not to look at the question on both sides. The question has its two sides. If the city be at some disadvantage in point of representation, it has great compensating advantages. It is the principal seat of legislation. Few people ever consider what an advantage this is. The advantage is simply enormous. For ten or twelve weeks the members of the General Assembly from all the towns are every day in familiar intercourse with Providence people. The influences exerted by this intercourse are incalculable, especially if there be any measure pending in the General Assembly in which the city has a strong interest. Many of these influences are the more potent because they reach the members indirectly, under the guise of social or friendly remark. There is also the more direct form of influence by lobbying, or by statement, testimony and argument before the legislative committees. The city enjoys great facilities in this respect from the presence of the Assembly. And finally, the city has, generally, in support of its interests, the united advocacy of the most powerful newspapers in the

State. I think it is not too much to say that these extrinsic advantages are worth more to the city than any proposed increase of her delegation would be, if the increase could only be secured by a surrender of them.

The city has twelve representatives. The general impression is, that her twelve have no more power than any other twelve. The impression is erroneous. Her twelve constitute a compact body, a self-marshalled phalanx, always ready to co-operate. In union there is strength; and when one of them speaks and the others echo his speech, the nucleus of a party is instantly formed, which rapidly gathers recruits from all sides. The Providence twelve are more powerful than any other twelve because they more readily combine when the city is interested. They resemble a solid battalion among an army of stragglers. Our fathers understood this and limited the representation of the city, as a salutary check upon her power, which would otherwise become exorbitant ; for they were of the opinion that power, decentralized, emanating from all parts of the State, is infinitely steadier and safer and wiser in its action than power concentrated in a single city. It has been said that Paris is France ; and it is because Paris is France that France is the theatre of continual convulsions and revolutions. Give Providence a representation in the two houses of the Assembly proportionate to her population, and, politically speaking, Providence will be Rhode Island. She will acquire a complete supremacy, and the other towns will be doomed to political insignificance. Now, much as I like the city, I do not think this is "a consummation devoutly to be wished." We want for the legislative work of the State the good practical common sense of the better minds of all the towns ; and certainly we cannot expect to get it if the towns are converted into the mere satellites of the city. But furthermore, equalization of representation and equalization of the suffrage go together. If either step be taken the other will pretty surely follow.

Take the two steps, and Providence will dominate the State with despotic sway, and Rhode Island will be what the State of New York would be, if, curtailed in territory, she were ruled by the city of New York, without the conservative reaction of her large rural population. I think we may confidently assume that our fathers were not the political idiots that they are represented to have been by men who cannot fathom the wisdom of their policy, but that they had good reasons, profound and statesman-like reasons, for what they did.

Another objection to the constitution attacks the provision which requires the payment of a dollar tax from all but real estate voters, as a prerequisite of the right to vote. The objection is to the registry tax, so called, —a tax which is assessed on registered voters, not otherwise taxed, and which they can pay or not at their option, but which, if it be not paid, they will have no right to vote. The constitution provides that the registry taxes of any town or city "shall be paid into the treasury of such town or city and be applied to the support of public schools therein." The rationale of the provision is evident. Our fathers thought that any citizen, worthy of the elective franchise, would have interest enough in the general welfare to be willing to pay a dollar a year for the public schools of his town or city, and that unless he evinced that degree of interest by paying the tax, he should not be allowed to vote. It is impossible to say that the provision, if it only operated according to its design, would not be wise and beneficent. Nothing will sooner develop a general interest in the State than to make a willing sacrifice for it ; for sacrifice is both seed and fruit as well of patriotism as of religion. Our fathers supposed that every voter was going to pay his own tax. They did not foresee that the office-seeker, for his own ends, would volunteer to pay it for him, and that thus an institution, which in its legitimate operation was calculated to cultivate a manly and intelligent public spirit,

would degenerate in practice into a mercenary system, under
which the voter would sell out his political birth-right for
the pettiest possible mess of pottage. The mischief did
not show itself at once; for at first the tax was required to
be paid in the calendar year preceding the election, and
the candidate for office would not pay it so long beforehand,
lest another, getting the nomination, might reap where he
had sown. The law was changed in 1851. The time of
payment was then deferred until within three days of election, and since then thousands of voters have learned to submit without shame to the degradation of having their registry
taxes paid for them, the payment has come to be regarded
as a regular part of the election expenses, and certain high
offices go, almost as a matter of course, to men who can
make or secure large contributions to the necessary fund.
And this, though bad enough, is not the worst; for the de-
scent is easy from such a practice to downright bribery and
corruption. I have long been of the opinion that the tax,
by its perversion, has become a prolific source of evil. I
have voted, and am ready to vote again, for its abolition.
But, while I condemn the tax, I cannot condemn the authors
of it. They meant it for good; and they are not to blame
because, while they clearly saw the good which would result
from its legitimate operation, they did not also foresee the
evil to which it might be perverted.

There are other objections made to the constitution which
I do not care to discuss. Amendments are also suggested,
some of which I should not be sorry to see adopted, if they
were constitutionally adopted. There are men, however,
who maintain that the constitution can be legally amended,
through the medium of a convention, without following the
deliberate and guarded methods prescribed in it, by a mere
majority vote of the people. On this point, which is to my
mind an exceedingly important point, I have something
which I wish to say.

In March, 1883, the senate of the State asked the judges

4

of the supreme court for their opinion on the subject; and
the judges gave it as their opinion that "the mode provided
in the constitution for the amendment thereof is the only
mode in which it can be constitutionally amended." Their
opinion was, that the power to amend being given in a particular mode, the particular mode is exclusive, any other being impliedly prohibited. They fortified themselves by authority, by considerations drawn from the character of the power,
and by the constitution itself. The opinion has excited some
adverse criticism and has been elaborately assailed by ex-Chief
Justice Bradley in the Providence *Journal* and *Press*. The
argument of Judge Bradley presents, so far as I know, every
objection which has been raised to the view taken by the
judges, and therefore I propose to examine it, saying what
I have to say in support of the view by way of counter argument. I shall endeavor to be brief, and, at the same time,
plain and simple, so that everybody can understand what I
say and can easily judge whether it be sound or sophistical.

Before I take up Judge Bradley's argument, I have a word
to say in regard to certain preliminary strictures on the judges
in which he has been pleased to indulge himself. The senate asked the judges for their opinion "without any unneces-
sary delay." They complied, giving their opinion six days
later. The judges, who were holding court all the while, in
announcing their opinion, expressed a regret that they had
not had an opportunity "for a more careful study." Judge
Bradley blames them for their expedition, and infers that
their opinion must have been given off-hand on a question
which was new to them, and that it may therefore be regarded as precipitate and ill-advised. I care nothing for the
censure, but I controvert the inference. To me, at least,
the question was not novel, though I had not given it any
special study; but, on the contrary, it had been known to
me ever since the time when, more than thirty years ago, I
heard the late Richard W. Greene, then Chief Justice of the
Supreme Court, denouncing a celebrated statesman of the

State of New York, for the active part which he had taken in amending the constitution of New York, through the medium of a convention, without following the method prescribed in it. Chief Justice Greene inveighed against the proceeding, in his emphatic way, characterizing it as a species of Dorrism. I have heard Judge Bradley speak of Chief Justice Greene, as a lawyer, with unstinted eulogy; and possibly because he was so great a lawyer, his remark sunk the more deeply into my mind, like a living seed for future germination. The opinion, however, was the opinion of five judges. I do not know what the experience of Judge Bradley may have been, but my experience is, that five independent minds do not reach a unanimous opinion on any debatable matter without a degree of consideration — a looking from various points of view—which saves it from being precipitate.

Judge Bradley next passes to a labored effort to show that the opinion of the judges is nothing but their opinion, and that the General Assembly has the same power to call a constitutional convention which it had before it was given. He professes to think that the judges themselves have somewhere advanced an exorbitant claim of authority for their opinions, though he confesses that they are not the chief offenders. I think the notion that they have offended at all is simply the coinage of his own too lively fancy. The only case that I know of in which the matter is so much as broached is *Taylor v. Place*, 4 R. I., 324, 330. The question there was, whether the General Assembly has judicial power, and the position was taken that the question was answered by the opinion of the judges, given at the request of the General Assembly, on the constitutionality of an act to reverse and annul the judgment for treason against Thomas W. Dorr, and was, therefore, to be regarded as *res adjudicata*. This position, however, was taken, not by the court nor by any of the judges, but by counsel, and, *mirabile dictu*, Judge Bradley was himself the counsel. Judge Bradley *now* distinguishes between a judgment of court and an opinion of the judges. He professes great reverence for the judges when they are deciding cases, but thinks they are entitled to no more respect than so many lawyers when they give an opinion. Doubtless his distinction is not unfounded, but nevertheless, I think he pushes it to an extreme. The judges are the constitutional advisers of the Governor and of the General Assembly; and, consequently, their opinions, given at the request of the Governor or of either house of the General Assembly, have more than an individual authority, being given in their public capacity under the sanction of their official oaths.

Judge Bradley makes the point that the question on which the opinion was given is political, not judicial, and argues that it is for the General Assembly to decide it for the judges, rather than for the judges to decide it for the General Assembly. I do not care to contest the point with him; but, conceding it, what follows? The question, whether political or not, is constitutional, and the members of the General Assembly are just as firmly bound by their oaths to support the constitution in dealing with a political, as they are in dealing with a legislative question. They have no absolution, however the matter may be regarded. The senators, realizing this, applied to the judges for their opinion, and the judges, as was their duty, gave it. Now, say the question was political, yet how does it follow that the opinion was either impertinent, erroneous or unworthy of regard? It seems to me that if the opinion be right, it is the duty of the members of the General Assembly to follow it. It seems to me further that, as a matter of conscience — though I am no casuist — it will be better for them to follow it until they are clearly satisfied that it is wrong. But if the opinion be clearly wrong, or if it has been conclusively refuted by Judge Bradley, I do not ask them to regard it, whether the question be political or non-political. What is the use of befogging a plain matter with irrelevant distinctions?

With these remarks on the preliminaries to Judge Bradley's argument, let us now proceed to the argument itself.
But here I encounter an embarrassment at the threshold.
Judge Bradley is a great legal luminary, and has an over-
powering reputation. Sometimes when, on a quiet morn-
ing, I open my Providence *Journal*, thinking only to read
the news or to enjoy the fine Addisonian humor of that ge-
nial sheet, I come plump on some learned lucubration from
his potent pen,* and, dipping into it cursorily here and
there, I immediately begin to feel as if I were reading, not
a dissertation or an argument, but a royal pronunciamento ;
the writer seems to be looking down from so lofty and se-
rene a height. The Judge is quite conscious of the advantage which his distinction gives him and does not disdain to
use it ; but on the contrary, whenever he discovers a lack of
weight in his argument, he promptly throws his reputation,
as a conqueror might throw his sword, into the ascending
scale. A notable instance of this occurred last winter at a
hearing before a committee of the General Assembly on constitutional changes. Judge Bradley appeared before the
committee, and, making a few remarks, handed to the members printed slips containing his argument. "In answer to
a question by Dr. Garvin," says the Providence *Journal*, in
its report of the hearing, "Judge Bradley said that the constitution did not impliedly or explicitly prohibit the holding
of a convention, but requires and confirms the right of the

---

* Not long ago, Judge Bradley contributed a series of articles to the *Journal*, reflecting
on the supreme court of the State for not giving in writing the grounds of its decision in
matters of fact. The articles contain many wise and valuable remarks which I have no
disposition to gainsay ; but the practice which they reprobate is not peculiar to the supreme court of Rhode Island. It prevails in other state courts and has been latterly
adopted in the supreme court of the United States. In *Tyler v. Campbell*, 106 U. S., 122,
Judge Gray states simply the conclusion of the court, and remarks that, as the case involves only a question of fact, " an extended opinion would not be according to the practice of the court and would serve no useful purpose." It may not be to the credit of the
judges of the supreme court of the United States, that they agree, where Judge Bradley
disagrees, with the judges of the supreme court of Rhode Island, but evidently they are
in that predicament.

Assembly to institute proceedings." The reader will remark the absolute assurance of his answer. He puts his foot upon the opinion of the five judges, as if it were simply an egg-shell, which he had only to step upon to crush it to atoms.

Now if Judge Bradley had come to a consideration of the question in a purely judicial temper of mind, I might myself be overawed by his dogmatic deliverances. He did not so come to it; his published argument was simply an elaborate defence of a conclusion to which he had committed himself thirty years before. In 1853, he was state senator for the town of North Providence. The General Assembly, at its May session for that year, passed an act providing for a convention to form a new constitution, subject, however, to the approval of the voters. At an election, held June 28, 1853, the voters, mindful of the lesson which they had learned in 1842, emphatically rejected the act by a vote of 4,570 for, to 6,282 against it. At its October session for that year, the General Assembly passed an act for a convention to revise the constitution, subject to the approval of the voters. At an election, held November 21, 1853, the act was rejected by a vote of 3,778 for, to 7,618 against it, an increase over the first vote too significant not to be understood. Judge Bradley was of the party that passed these acts, and voted for them. No man can detach himself from his antecedents. The argument of 1883 was the natural sequel to the vote of 1853.

But Judge Bradley once more committed himself still more deeply to the same view. At its January session, 1854, the Assembly passed an act reversing and annulling the judgment of the supreme court against Thomas W. Dorr for treason, and ordering the record of it to be cancelled. Judge Bradley voted for the act. The reader who remembers his profession of reverence for the judiciary, in the exercise of its purely judicial functions, will be surprised; for it was not an opinion of the judges, but a judgment of court, which was subjected to this unprecedented indignity. I leave the reader to his own commentary; my purpose is simply to show Judge Bradley's attitude toward the question under debate. The doctrine of Dorr was this: that a majority of the people have the right to change their constitution at any time and in any way, with or without law. A vote for the act was virtually a vote for that doctrine; and of course any person who voted for it would be pretty sure to accept the milder doctrine of Judge Bradley's argument.

I think, therefore, that I have shown that Judge Bradley is strongly committed to the conclusion for which he contends; and consequently that I have a right to ask the reader not to trust him blindly on account of his reputation, but rather, considering his argument as an argument in favor of a foregone conclusion, to examine it on its merits. If he will grant me this, I will ask him for nothing further except his careful attention to what follows.

The following is the provision of the constitution for the amendment thereof, viz.:

The general assembly may propose amendments to this constitution by the votes of a majority of all the members elected to each house. Such propositions for amendment shall be published in the newspapers, and printed copies of them shall be sent by the secretary of State, with the names of all the members who shall have voted thereon, with the yeas and nays, to all the town and city clerks in the State. The said propositions shall be, by said clerks, inserted in the warrants or notices by them issued, for warning the next annual town and ward meetings in April; and the clerks shall read said propositions to the electors when thus assembled, with the names of all the representatives and senators who shall have voted thereon, with the yeas and nays, before the election of senators and representatives shall be had. If a majority of all the members elected to each house, at said annual meeting, shall approve any proposition thus made, the same shall be published and submitted to the electors in the mode provided in the act of approval; and if then approved by three-fifths of the electors of the State present, and voting thereon in town and ward meetings, it shall become a part of the constitution of the State.

The constitution, in Article IV, Section 1, declares: "This constitution shall be the supreme law of the State, and any law inconsistent therewith shall be void."

The judges, in their opinion, yielding to this declaration, maintained that the constitution having provided a mode for its own amendment, the enactment of any different mode by the General Assembly would be void. The correctness of this proposition seems, at first blush, too plain for controversy. Its opponents attempt to controvert it in this way: The constitution, they argue, though it provides a particular mode of amendment, does not prohibit amendment in other modes, and therefore an amendment through the medium of a constitutional convention, without following the provision, is valid. The argument, it will be observed, rests on the assumption that the power cannot be deemed to have been prohibited to the General Assembly, because it is not prohibited by words of express negation. The judges, in their opinion, did not assent to this assumption; and very clearly the assumption is unfounded, unless the power differs .in this respect from any other legislative power. The constitution, Article IV, Section 2, declares: "The legislative power, under this constitution, shall be vested in two houses, the one to be called the senate, the other the house of representatives; and both together, the General Assembly." What is granted is, not legislative omnipotence, but "the legislative power *under this constitution*," and, under the constitution, the legislative power is confessedly limited in many ways, not only expressly but by implication. For example, the General Assembly cannot take away the right of trial by jury in common law actions or in criminal cases. The constitution, however, does not declare that the General Assembly shall *not* take the right away. It only declares that "the right of trial by jury shall remain inviolate," and from this affirmative language the prohibition is implied. Other examples could be given. Now the judges, applying this principle, held that a particular mode of amendment being prescribed, any other mode was prohibited by implication, although no prohibitory language was employed.

Such a construction in the matter of a statute, will or deed is very common. The reader is doubtless familiar with it as applied to a mortgage deed with power of sale. The power is generally given to be exercised in a particular way, as, e. g., at auction after advertisement: and it has frequently been decided that a sale in any other way is invalid. Such a decision has nothing arbitrary in it, but follows the familiar usages of language. If a farmer lends his horse to his neighbor, telling him how to use it, he does not think it necessary to prohibit his using it differently, the prohibition being implied; for he cannot use it differently, if he does as he is told. The old Roman jurists saw this centuries ago, as clearly as we see it to-day, and accordingly laid down the rule, "*expressio unius est exclusio alterius*,"* which is as much a rule of our law as of theirs. The judges, in their opinion, apply this rule to the constitution for the purpose of getting at its meaning; and certainly if any instrument ought to be construed according to the common usages of human speech, a constitution, adopted by the people as the expression of their sovereign will, ought to be so construed, unless there is some reason, historic or other, for construing it otherwise.

Now let us consider the reasons which Judge Bradley opposes to this construction. His first reason is that the rule applied by the judges, however applicable it may be in private matters, is not applicable to limit the sovereign power, or in other words, that the power of the people, including their power to amend their form of government, cannot be limited by implication. The wide-awake reader will here detect a specimen of the logical legerdemain which is sometimes resorted to by the skillful advocate. The judges maintained that the constitution having provided one

* The rule literally translated is: " The expression of one [way or thing] is the exclusion of any other," or less literally translated, " When one [way or thing] is expressly directed, any other is impliedly prohibited."

5

mode of amendment, the General Assembly could not provide another, their power being limited by implication. Judge Bradley, adroitly substituting the people for the Assembly, replies that the power of the people cannot be limited by implication. Why does he make the substitution? He makes it because he knows that the power of the Assembly can be limited by implication, and is so limited in our constitution. He has some excuse, however; for if the Assembly is shut up to the mode expressly provided, the people are also shut up to it, since the people cannot move in the matter of an amendment without the initiative of the Assembly. But though this may be some excuse for the substitution, it does not justify it: for after all, if the limitation is implied, it is the Assembly whose power is limited, and it is the people who limit it, not to their own detriment, but for their own protection against hasty and ill-considered changes. I must ask the reader to remember this; but at the same time I shall not refuse to meet Judge Bradley on his own ground. The assertion that the sovereign power of the people cannot be limited by implication has so imposing a sound that the unwary reader might easily be led to accept it as a legal aphorism; but, nevertheless, I venture to deny it, and to call for authority in support of it.

Judge Bradley has adduced what he claims to be authority. Let us examine it. In the first place, he adduces a rule laid down in Dwarris on Statutes, that "the rights of the crown can never be taken away by doubtful words or ambiguous expressions, but only by *express terms*." The rule is, perhaps, stated a little strongly, but taking it as stated, and conceding that what is true of the crown in England is true of the people here, how does the rule bear on the question under debate? The question here does not relate to the taking away of right or power, but to its voluntary renunciation. In this country the sovereign power, which resides in the people, cannot be taken away by anybody but the people, acting either directly or by representation. It is not laid down in Dwarris that a royal or a public grant admits of no implication against the grantor. A royal or public grant is construed like a private grant, except that in ambiguous matters it is construed the more favorably to the grantor, whereas a private grant is construed the more favorably to the grantee. This does not help Judge Bradley; for here the Assembly is the grantee, and the rule tells against its having the power to initiate amendments otherwise than as provided. There is authority, if Judge Bradley wants it, which is more in point. The federal constitution is an instrument by which the States granted certain powers to the United States. There was formerly a school of statesmen known as strict constructionists. They insisted that the States had parted with no powers except such as were expressly granted and such as were necessarily incident to the grant; for even they admitted that incidental powers might be implied. In one matter they took the same position which Judge Bradley takes. They maintained that the States, though they had united to form the union, had never *expressly* agreed that the union should be indissoluble, and that, therefore, the States being sovereign except in so far as they had voluntarily abridged their sovereignty, any State, if it thought it had cause, had a right to secede, since its power could not be limited by implication. Certain States holding this doctrine acted on it. We all know what followed. The doctrine was confuted on the battlefield. It was disaffirmed by the courts. And it seems to me that, since then, the idea that the sovereign power of the people cannot be limited by an implication resulting from the language in which the people have expressed their will, ought to be regarded as too thoroughly discredited to find place anywhere out of the limbo of exploded errors.

Judge Bradley also quotes from Dwarris the following remark in support of his position, to wit: "Affirmative words do not take away the common law, a former custom or a preceding statute." I can imagine the reader, as he reads this, wondering what bearing it has on the question here ; for how, he may ask himself, can the General Assembly, which is the creature of the constitution, have any right independently of it, either at common law or by a former custom or a preceding statute. The doctrine, I seem to hear him say, is not only strange but dangerous, for if it amounts to anything, it amounts to this, that there is one constitution, written and ordained by the people, and another, unwritten and apochryphal, which the General Assembly is left to evolve for itself out of a sort of hypothetical nebula of custom and common law. Such a doctrine is convenient for a legislature when it finds itself hampered by the written constitution ; but can it be that this is what Judge Bradley intends? Probably not. The man who originates an erroneous doctrine for a particular purpose, seldom intends all the consequences which follow from it. He is too intent on his purpose to discover them.

Judge Bradley, however, explains himself in these words : "The right here in question exists by the common law of the constitutions of American States, as we have seen by former custom of this and other States." The explanation is remarkable. It may be well enough to call the practice in regard to constitutional changes "a common law ;" but it is the merest figure of speech to call it so, and to found an argument on it as if it were a fact is a most egregious fallacy. The constitution is, to use its own words, "the supreme law of the State," and it cannot therefore be subject to alteration by any common law right. The real fact is this, that the General Assembly has no power except that which the people, which it represents, have conferred upon it, either expressly or impliedly, in the constitution. Judge Bradley virtually admits this later in his argument. The judges, in their opinion, had said that, in the absence of any express provision, the General Assembly would have the power to initiate constitutional changes *ex necessitate* by implication and without restriction. Judge Bradley, correcting this, declares that the power is a legislative power included in the general grant. Doubtless this is the better view; but it is inconsistent with the supposition that the General Assembly has the power, independently of the constitution, at common law, and it is fatal to the argument founded upon it.

Judge Bradley's purpose in the correction, however, was not to undermine his own argument, but to controvert the opinion of the judges. "There is, therefore," he says, "no room for any implied prohibition, for there is an express grant of the power in question by a general grant of legislative powers, which includes it." The argument is untenable. It does not follow that the power is unlimited because it is included in the general grant, nor that the power, being included in the general grant, is not limited by force of the special provision, because it would be unlimited without it. What is called the general grant is not an unlimited grant; for, as we have already seen, what is granted to the General Assembly by the constitution is not legislative omnipotence, but "the legislative power under this constitution," the power being thus subjected to all the limitations of the constitution, express or implied, by the terms of the grant. I do not mean to concede that the words "under this constitution" were necessary to accomplish this; but they make plainer, if possible, what would be perfectly plain without them. The power is conferred in a single clause. The limitations are distributed under their appropriate heads through the constitution. This could not be otherwise without a clumsiness of composition which would probably introduce more ambiguities than it would remove. It is for the reader to interpret the power in the light of its limitations, bringing them together. If we do so in this matter, we shall have the constitution reading in legal effect as follows: The legislative power, including the power to provide for changes of the constitution, shall be vested in the General Assembly, but the General Assembly, when it proposes amendments, shall, etc., using the language of the special provision. Now can there be any doubt that if the power were so given, the General Assembly would be limited in the exercise of it to the mode prescribed? The power is so given in legal effect, though the literary plan of the constitution requires that the grant of the power, as included in the general grant, shall be expressed in one place, and the mode of exercising it prescribed in another. The general grant and the special provision are both parts of the same great ordinance, and must be construed, not consecutively and separately, but simultaneously and together.

I come now to a point which I think did not receive the prominence it is entitled to in the opinion of the judges. Implications are of two kinds. An implication may be necessary and conclusive, or it may be merely reasonable and liable to be controlled by counter considerations. I have so far discussed the question here without regard to this distinction. I now maintain that the implication for which I contend is necessary and conclusive. I will ask the reader to revert to the provision in regard to amendments, and study it a moment. It begins by giving the General Assembly leave to propose amendments. The language is purely permissive. The Assembly may or may not propose, as it chooses. If, however, it chooses to propose, the provision goes on to prescribe the steps which are to be taken. There is an instant change in the form of expression. The language ceases to be permissive and becomes peremptory. It is not *may*, but *shall*, *shall*, *shall*, with imperative reiteration through all the steps of the procedure. Not only is the mode marked out, but the Assembly is *commanded* to follow it. Can the Assembly, then, depart from this mode and proceed in a different mode—in a mode which is different not only in some of the minor details, which may possibly be regarded as merely directory, but in the essential matters, in the principal directions which were designed to insure deliberation and an assured majority—can the Assembly, I say, thus depart from the prescribed mode consistently with it? If it cannot, the implication that it must not is necessary and conclusive. Indeed, if it cannot, the constitution does not leave the prohibition to a mere implication, but, as before quoted, it has itself declared, "this constitution shall be the supreme law of the State, and any law inconsistent therewith shall be void." I confidently affirm, therefore, that any mode provided by the General Assembly which materially differs from the mode prescribed in the constitution must necessarily be void. The people have legislated for themselves, and the Assembly cannot supersede or repeal their legislation by legislating differently. I will not multiply words; the demonstration is manifest without them.

Judge Bradley is evidently sensible of the strength of this position; for, unless I misapprehend his meaning, he attempts to avoid it in part by taking the ground that the constitutional provision relates only to amendments, and does not extend to the adoption of a new constitution. The judges, in their opinion, anticipating that such a distinction might be attempted, though unrecognized in 1853, answer it by saying in effect that it is a distinction without a difference, inasmuch as the adoption of a new constitution would be but an amendment under another form. "The power in a legislature to amend an act of legislation," says Judge Bradley, "does not exclude the power to repeal the act and make a new one. So the power in a government to amend its constitution, as occasion may require, does not exclude the power to reconstruct it anew, as occasion may require." The statement, taken literally, is in my opinion correct. Nobody has ever said that a power to amend a statute excludes the power to re-enact it, or that a power to amend the constitution excludes the power to reconstruct it. What the judges maintained was, and what I maintain is, that if the power to amend is limited by the constitution, either expressly or impliedly, to a particular mode, the amendment cannot be constitutionally effected in any other mode, even though it be proposed under the form of a new constitution. Judge Bradley does not squarely meet this proposition; though he evidently intends to have his readers suppose that he both meets and refutes it by making, in his solemn way, the indisputable statement just quoted.

He does assert, however, that the power to amend and the power to reconstruct are different, and therefore I presume that he intends to argue that it does not follow, because the power to amend is limited to a particular mode, that the power to reconstruct is either likewise limited or else excluded. Let us suppose that this is his argument, and that his statement was intended to support it. The statement contains two sentences. The first sentence is illustrative. As such let us consider it. There are two ways in which a statute can be amended. It can be patched by an amendatory act, or it can be re-enacted with the amendment incorporated. Now let us suppose that the constitution says of a particular statute, that, if amended, it shall be amended in a particular way, as e. g., by a two-thirds vote. In such case, according to Judge Bradley's argument, the statute, though not constitutionally amendable in the first mentioned manner without a two-thirds vote, may be constitutionally amended in the other manner by a mere majority vote, because in the other manner there is a new act, and the power of the Assembly to pass a new act is not excluded. Does Judge Bradley suppose that such an argument would satisfy any decent court in Christendom? I am quite sure that any decent court would say that the new act was nothing but the old act amended, and that it could not sanction such an attempt to circumvent the constitution.

It is precisely the same in regard to constitutional changes. A new constitution, if adopted, would be nothing but the old constitution amended. If a convention to frame a new constitution were called to-morrow, it could do nothing, even though Dr. Garvin himself were there to recommend every nostrum of his political pharmacopœia, but introduce a few alterations and additions which might just as well be introduced by the specially prescribed method of amendment.

Doubtless there is a formal difference. There is also a technical difference, inasmuch as a new constitution, considered as such, supersedes the old when it goes into effect, and probably, therefore, would have to make provision for continuing the old government until a new government could be formed under it. This, however, is merely incidental to change in that form, and does not alter the nature of the change itself, or make it any the less essentially an amendment. The word "amendment," as used in the constitution, denotes the change introduced or to be introduced, not the process of introduction. A glance at the provision will show this. The word should not be narrowed by technical distinctions or frittered away by nice refinements. It should be interpreted in the light of its context, and so interpreted the largeness of its meaning becomes too distinct for doubt ; for the context clearly manifests a conservative purpose which would be frustrated by the narrower interpretation for which Judge Bradley contends.

Judge Bradley seems to have an idea that a new constitution would have to be framed by a convention, and that for that reason it would have some special virtue in it distinguishing it from an amendment. But why a convention is necessary, or what is the nature of that virtue which it can impart, he does not tell us, and I confess I cannot conjecture. A convention simply prepares the draft of a new constitution, as a scrivener prepares the draft of a will ; but it is the vote of the people duly taken in the one case, as it is the signature of the testator duly attested in the other, which gives vitality to the instrument. And as the testator can dispense with the scrivener, if he can get his will without him, so can the people dispense with a convention, if they can get a constitution which suits them without it. A legislative committee can do the work just as well ;—the only superiority which a convention has being this, that being chosen by the people to prepare a draft, it is perhaps a little likelier to prepare a draft which will suit them. A convention is simply an agency : it has no original power; it can do only what it is authorized to do by the act which calls it into being. The General Assembly and the people can do without it whatever they can do through the medium of it, for they are the real powers. The practice of calling it is nothing but a usage which may be followed by, but which cannot control, the law-making power. I do not think that even Judge Bradley himself will say that a new constitution, which has been otherwise duly adopted, would be invalid simply because it was not drafted and proposed through the medium of a convention.

But if this be so, what follows under the distinction which is attempted between amending and reconstructing the constitution ? This, namely : that the General Assembly, though it cannot provide for an amendment in the usual form without following the constitutional provision, can nevertheless provide for an amendment in the form of a new constitution independently of it, submitting the new constitution for adoption on approval by a bare majority of the qualified voters ; or even, according to some precedents, by a bare majority of those who would or could be qualified under it, if adopted. Was there ever a more preposterous conclusion ? A convention if called would afford some slender protection against inconsiderate action by waking public attention, but, as we see, even that is at the mercy of the General Assembly. What, then, if Judge Bradley's views prevail, becomes of the conservatism which our fathers, knowing the political excitability of small States, were so anxious to insure ? It vanishes like a vapor. It was not until after our constitution was adopted that the views now supported by Judge Bradley were anywhere accepted, and I am quite sure that our fathers never anticipated them. I am sure, too, that they had no reason to anticipate them. When I say this, however, I do not mean to say that the General Assembly cannot call a convention to prepare amendments, or even to prepare them in the form of a new constitution, but I mean to say this only: that such amendments, by whomsoever or in whatever form prepared, cannot be constitutionally adopted unless they are proposed and approved in accordance with the special provision of the constitution. An amendment in the form of a new constitution can easily be so proposed and approved by prefixing to it the words: "The constitution shall be so amended as to read as follows, to wit;" and probably even, without them, by simply styling it an amendment in the procedure.

I pass to another point. Judge Bradley contends that the constitution explicitly authorizes changes otherwise than in the mode which is specially prescribed. For this he cites Section 1, of Article 1, which follows:

SECTION 1. In the words of the Father of his Country, we declare, that, "the basis of our political systems is the right of the people to make and alter their constitutions of government; but that the constitution which at any time exists, till changed by an explicit and authentic act of the whole people, is sacredly obligatory upon all."

This section purports to be, not a grant of power, but a declaration of right. It is very general in its terms. It was doubtless inserted to justify the change which was then making, as well as to assert the right to make future changes. It was inserted, moreover, in lieu of a section offered and rejected, which affirmed, or was supposed to affirm, the Dorr doctrine, and, without doubt, its principal purpose was to disaffirm that doctrine. Hence the words, " the constitution which at any time exists, till changed by an explicit and authentic act of the whole people, is sacredly obligatory upon all." Judge Bradley contends that the meaning is that the people have the right to change the constitution by a mere majority vote, if they only do it through the medium of a convention and under an act of the General Assembly. I agree that it means this in its retrospective application ; for our fathers proceeded in that manner when they adopted the present constitution ; but they were not then restrained by any special provision ; and it does not follow that we can now proceed in the same manner, under a constitution which has such a provision. We must construe the section and the provision together, and, so construing them, I do not find anything in the section which is inconsistent with the provision, taking the provision as I interpret it. The section declares that the existing constitution remains obligatory "till changed by an explicit and authentic act of the whole people." There are two requirements here. First, the act must be authentic ; and second, it must be the act of the whole people. To meet these requirements, the act must be performed under the sanction of the law, for otherwise it cannot be legally authenticated, nor be the act of the whole people, if any portion of them dissent. The vote of any number less than all cannot be the vote of the whole people, even in contemplation of law, unless it is legally and constitutionally given. It is not enough, therefore, that the change is effected under an act of the General Assembly, unless the act is constitutional. An unconstitutional statute is a nullity. We are thus brought back to the very question which I have already so fully argued, namely: whether an act which purports to provide for a change of the constitution in any manner other than that which is prescribed in the special provision, is constitutional. I maintain, for reasons which I need not repeat, that such an act, being inconsistent with the special provision, is unconstitutional and void. It follows that the only mode in which our constitution can be changed by "an explicit and authentic act of the whole people" is the mode prescribed in the special provision.

Judge Bradley also cites Section 10, of Article IV, which reads as follows : " The General Assembly shall continue to exercise the powers they have heretofore exercised unless prohibited by this constitution." He contends that, since the Assembly exercised the power in question under the old charter, it can continue to exercise it under this section. Doubtless it can, unless prohibited; but since it cannot exercise the power in any other than the prescribed mode, consistently with the prescribed mode, it is prohibited by implication; and indeed, under the clause which declares that any law inconsistent with the constitution shall be void, it is prohibited, if not expressly, at least as unequivocally as if it were expressly prohibited. In *Taylor* v. *Place*, 4 R. I., 324, the Supreme Court decided that an implied is as effectual as an express prohibition. Judge Bradley attempts to limit the authority of *Taylor* v. *Place*, but the attempt, contrary to his wont, is rather blind, and it is certainly not successful. The idea that the exercise of the power can be prohibited only by express negation is utterly untenable. For if it were tenable, mark the result: the General Assembly, under the old charter, was accustomed to exercise power over the right of suffrage, restricting or extending it. It is nowhere prohibited by express negation from continuing to exercise the power; but certainly no one, not a fanatic nor a fool, will have the effrontery to maintain that it can continue still to exercise it. There is a kind of reasoning which the logicians call a *reductio ad absurdum*, which consists in showing that a proposition must be erroneous because it is absurd. It seems clear to my mind that the proposition which I am combating is of that character.

I will now briefly consider the precedents which Judge Bradley adduces. And here I will premise that I admit that a legislature can provide for constitutional changes, to be effected by a mere majority vote, if the constitution contains no restrictive provision. The Judges in their opinion do not deny this. Precedents for such changes are therefore not in point. There is no particular mode to follow, if there be none prescribed. Judge Bradley, however, mentions seven states in which as many constitutions, having special provisions for amendment, have been changed with-

out following those provisions. These are pertinent. But
what is their value as precedents? Judge Bradley thinks
they are of great value; I value them less highly. I will
state the reasons why I value them less highly.

In the first place, we have only the instances in which such
changes have been adopted. We are not told how often
such changes have been rejected, when proposed, because
unconstitutional. Probably the precedents, if we only
knew, are as numerous on the one side as on the other. In
the second place, the constitutions of the several States
have their differences as well as their resemblances, and
what is wrong under one may be right under another. The
special provision which is so clearly mandatory in our constitution may be less clearly so in another, or it may be
accompanied by some other clause which countervails its
restrictive effect. If the declaratory clause, which was
offered and rejected in the convention which framed our
constitution, had been adopted, we should find it difficult to
maintain that the special provision is exclusive and controlling. In some of the instances mentioned by Judge Bradley,
the constitutions contained such or similar clauses.

I admit, however, that among the cases of constitutional
change cited by him, there are cases which "go on all fours"
as precedents in his favor. Now what have I to say of
them? I have this to say, that the legislature of no other
State can decide for the people of Rhode Island what is the
meaning of their constitution, or absolve them from their
duty to support and obey it according to the meaning which
it has in Rhode Island. A legislative precedent is not like
a judicial precedent, for legislatures give no reasons for
their decisions, and we cannot know what arguments or influences may have prevailed with them. I desire to speak
respectfully and without offence, but nevertheless I must
say that in my opinion a legislature is not generally well
fitted to decide legal or constitutional questions. Statutes
are frequently enacted which the courts pronounce uncon-

stitutional. Moreover, questions of constitutional change are apt to be party questions. When the party in power favors a change, it naturally wishes to accomplish it, and it easily persuades itself that what it wishes done can be constitutionally done. This is human nature. The disposition shows itself even in matters which are not immoderately exciting; and we all know that when party zeal is inflamed, fanaticism getting the better of reason, constitutional scruples melt like wax, and men of strong mind even, catching the common contagion, cease to think for themselves and rush recklessly along with their fellows. In such circumstances, the example of one State is all too eagerly followed in another. One illustration of this, history has blazoned in letters of living light. On December 20, 1860, South Carolina passed her ordinance of secession, setting an example which was instantly followed by six other States, and by still four more within a few months. We have here a series of precedents which, since they were set, have been too decisively overruled to be any longer cited as authority; and yet it so happens that five of the seven States, whose action Judge Bradley considers so worthy of imitation, were also five of the eleven that seceded.

I have said that Judge Bradley values this class of precedents more highly than I do. I think I can safely add, judging from the past, that he values them more highly than does the State of Rhode Island. Hitherto Rhode Island has led her sisters oftener than she has followed them. It is her glory that she began her career by leading the world. I do not believe she has ever repented of her independence. On the contrary, I have the faith to think that she remains true to her historic character; and that, while she respectfully considers the example of her sisters, she will not blindly follow it; but that, after carefully weighing all reasons and counter reasons, all arguments and counter arguments, she will, now as of old, shoulder the responsibility of thinking and deciding for herself.

The question under debate has never, to my knowledge, been the subject of authoritative adjudication. The explanation of this is simple. Constitutional changes, effected through the medium of a convention, have generally, if not always, been effected by the adoption of a new constitution. A new constitution is not like a new statute. If a statute be unconstitutionally enacted, the court, whenever the statute is brought into litigation, pronounces it null and void. But if a new constitution is established, resulting in the establishment of a new government, with the assent of the old, the change, though unconstitutional and revolutionary, is nevertheless effectual, and it cannot be reversed, within the State, without a counter revolution. This is because the old government, betraying its trust, will have abdicated its functions and consented to its own dissolution, and can, therefore, no longer support the old constitution; and the new government, including the judiciary, having taken office under the new constitution and sworn to support it, cannot consistently entertain the question of its legitimacy. The change amounts to a revolution, peacefully accomplished.

A few cases are, however, cited by Judge Bradley, in which the question has been incidentally mooted or considered. The cases are *Wells* v. *Bain*, 75 Penn. St. 39; Wood's Appeal, *ibid*, 59; *Collier, Governor,* v. *Frierson*, 24 Alabama, 100; *Koehler & Lange* v. *Hill*, 60 Iowa, 545.

I will first consider the Pennsylvania cases. The Pennsylvanians, it seems, adopted a new constitution in place of a former one, containing a provision for its own amendment, without following that provision. But the former one contained, besides the provision, a declaration that the people "have at all times an inalienable and indefeasible right to alter, reform or abolish their government in such manner as they may think proper." The declaration does not differ much from that which was offered in our constitutional convention and there rejected.* In *Wells* v. *Bain*, the court was of opinion that this declaration, taken in connection with the declaration of the right of popular petition, authorized the passage of an act providing for the formation of a new constitution through the medium of a convention, without following the special provision. The court, however, does not seem to have considered whether the provision had any restrictive effect, but it seems to have decided the question precisely as it would have decided it if there had been no provision. Moreover, the question was not, so far as appears, either raised or controverted in the suit, the question in the suit being whether the convention, its lawfulness being assumed, could exercise original legislative power. The opinion of the court on this point, therefore, even if it can be regarded as more than a mere *dictum*, cannot be regarded as authoritative.

In Wood's Appeal, the question was more distinctly raised. The case originated in an inferior court. The opinion of that court is reported *in extenso*. It is this opinion which furnishes Judge Bradley, very largely, with his judicial thunder. The opinion, however, rests heavily on the declaration of right, and, while it recognizes the true point, nevertheless wanders off for authority to changes initiated or effected under constitutions which had no provisions for their own amendment, and finally reaches the conclusion that there is a principle underlying the whole American system, which authorizes constitutional changes, through the medium of a convention, unless expressly prohibited, whether there be any other mode of amendment provided in the constitution or not. The theory is, if I understand the opinion, that the power to change the con-

---

* The rejected section declared that, " The people have an inalienable and indefeasible right, in their original sovereign and unlimited capacity, to ordain and institute government, and in the same capacity to alter, reform, and totally change the same, whenever their safety or happiness requires."

stitution exists independently of the constitution, by usage
or custom or natural right. The theory is identical with
one of Judge Bradley's theories, which I have considered
and which, I think, I have shown to be chimerical. At any
rate, it is inconsistent with our constitution; for, let me
repeat, our constitution cannot be the supreme law, if there
be any law independent of it, by virtue of which it can
be altered or superseded. Judge Bradley says the opinion
of the inferior court was sustained by the supreme court
of Pennsylvania. This is an error. The case was carried
to the supreme court, but before it was reached for hearing, the new constitution had been adopted, and the
supreme court said : "The change made by the people in
their political institutions, by the adoption of the proposed
constitution, since this decree, forbids an inquiry into the
merits of this case. *The question is no longer judicial.*" The
supreme court, however, while it refrained from considering
this point, was not quite so non-committal on another. The
lower court had promulgated a wild and extravagant theory
in regard to the powers of constitutional conventions. The
supreme court dissects and demolishes this theory in a manner which, to say the least, will not add to the reputation of
its author, as a wise and trustworthy guide on questions of
constitutional law. The reader will observe, too, if he com-
pares these Pennsylvania cases, that the two courts, when
they agree in result, disagree in their reasons. Such a dis-
agreement is symptomatic of error.

In the Alabama case the supreme court held the following language : "We entertain no doubt that, to change the
constitution in any other mode than by a convention, every
requisition which is demanded by the instrument itself must
be observed, and the omission of any one is fatal to the
amendment." Judge Bradley finds a crumb of comfort in
the words, "in any other mode than by a convention," from
which he infers, perhaps a little too readily, that the court
would have sustained the amendment, if made through the

medium of a convention, even though it did not meet the
requirements of the constitution. I have already discussed
this view, and need not repeat myself. It rests on the idea
that a convention gets from the legislature or from the
people, or from the legislature and the people, in some
mysterious way, a power which neither the legislature nor
the people, nor the legislature and the people both together,
have without it. Such a doctrine savors of miracle or nec-
romancy, and it is at any rate too transcendental for me;
for whatever other merit it may have, it lacks the sovereign
merit of common sense. The Iowa case is like the Alabama
case, leaving out the intimation in regard to a convention.
So far as it goes, it is against Judge Bradley, and he does
not admire it.

I have a few words to say in regard to the opinion of the
judges of the supreme judicial court of Massachusetts, cited
by the judges of the supreme court of this State, as confirm-
atory of their views. Judge Bradley tries to explain it
away. I do not think he succeeds. The question pro-
pounded to the Massachusetts judges was: "Can any
specific and particular amendment or amendments be made
in any other manner than that prescribed in the ninth article of the amendments adopted in 1820?" Their answer
was: "Under and pursuant to the existing constitution,
there is no authority given by any reasonable construction
or necessary implication, by which any specific and particular amendment or amendments of the constitution can be
made in any other manner than that prescribed in the ninth
article of the amendments adopted in 1820." That is all
there is of the opinion which is pertinent here. It is short,
but in Mercutio's phrase, "it is enough." Judge Bradley
cannot parry it. It leaves him without any ground to stand
upon but this:—that though an amendment cannot be constitutionally made in the form of an amendment in any
other than the prescribed mode, it can be constitutionally
made independently of that mode, if you only put it in the

form of a new constitution and call it reconstruction. My opinion is that the grand old Massachusetts Chief Justice would have made short work with that argument, if he had had occasion to consider it.

Judge Bradley claims Daniel Webster as authority for him. The claim, however, is simply conjectural. Mr. Webster, in his great speech in *Luther* v. *Borden*, controverted the Dorr doctrine, and maintained that the people of a State cannot lawfully change their constitution without proceeding according to some law previously enacted. In support of this proposition he instanced the unbroken practice of the States from the Revolution down, referring particularly to New York, which had then but just accomplished such a change, as the last. Judge Bradley shows that the change in New York was effected by the adoption of a new constitution in place of one previously existing, which contained a special provision for its own amendment, and that the change, though effected under a legislative act, was not effected in pursuance of the provision. Hence, he infers that Mr. Webster, in citing the change, meant to indorse it as legitimate in that respect. The inference is clearly illogical. Mr. Webster's only purpose was to show that it had been the invariable practice of the people of the several States to wait for a statute providing for the change before making it; or, in other words, to show that the action of Dorr and his party was contrary to usage and without precedent. He cited the change in New York as an example of the practice, dwelling on it because it was the last. It was enough for his purpose that the people there had not taken the initiative, like Dorr and his party, but had waited for a statute. He did not consider — it was foreign to his purpose to consider — whether the statute was constitutional. The change had been accomplished, and, being a statesman as well as a lawyer, he would say nothing directly to disturb it. He was a great jurist, but he was also a great advocate, and as such he would not needlessly provoke antagonism on an irrelevant point.* And he could, with the better conscience, keep silence here, because he had already expressed himself on the point in an entirely inoffensive manner. Accordingly, I not only deny the correctness of Judge Bradley's claim, but on the strength of the expressions in the passage referred to, I claim Mr. Webster as an authority on my side. I will quote the passage in full, that the reader may judge of it :

"I have said that it is one principle of the American system that the people limit their governments, national and state. They do so; but it is another principle, equally true and certain, and, according to my judgment of things, equally important, that the people often *limit themselves*. They set bounds to their own power. They have chosen to secure the institutions which they establish against the sudden impulses of mere majorities. All our institutions teem with instances of this. It was their great conservative principle, in constituting forms of government, that they should secure what they had established against hasty changes by simple majorities. By the fifth article of the constitution of the United States, congress, two-thirds of both houses concurring, may propose amendments of the constitution ; or, on the application of the legislatures of two-thirds of the States, may call a convention ; and amendments proposed in either of these forms, must be ratified by the legislatures or conventions of three-fourths of the States. The fifth article of the constitution, if it was made a topic for those who framed "the people's constitution " of Rhode Island, could only have been a matter of reproach. It gives no countenance to any of these proceedings, or to anything like them. On the contrary, it is one remarkable instance of the enactment and application of that great American principle, that the constitution of government should be cautiously and prudently interfered with, and that changes should not ordinarily be begun and carried through by bare majorities."

I want the reader to study these pregnant sentences. Mr. Webster says the people limit themselves. He says they secure the forms of government which they establish from hasty changes by simple majorities. He tells us that this is their great conservative principle. But how do they secure their forms of government from hasty changes by simple majorities? He shows how, by referring to the provision for

* Judge Bradley has himself told us that the court was " composed principally of judges of a different school of political thought from Mr. Webster."

amendment in the constitution of the United States. That provision, so far as quoted by him, is, like ours, simply an affirmative provision. Is it not clear, then, that his meaning is, that the people secure their forms of government from hasty changes by simple majorities by prescribing modes of amendment which require the consent of more than simple majorities? That is evidently what he means. He mentions no other way, and, so far as I know, there was no other way in which such security was made in any State constitution. Judge Bradley may say that he speaks of the constitution of the United States. Certainly he does; but he speaks of State constitutions too; and he simply holds up the federal constitution as the common type or exemplar, by way of illustration, because it is more universally familiar than any State constitution. Any candid mind reading the passage as a whole must so construe it. The language is full of plural forms, and it refers, not exclusively, to any one, but to all the governments and constitutions, national and state, which belong to the American system. Judge Bradley, in his zeal, would utterly empty the language of its significance. The reader, I trust, will not follow him. He will give plain words their plain meanings, and moreover, catching inspiration from the great spirit which breathes through them, he will interpret them not in any carping and hypercritical temper, but in the large and sagacious but conservative temper in which they were uttered.

There is an old maxim which in Latin reads, *Contemporanea expositio est optima*, and which in English means that contemporaneous construction is best. The reason for it is obvious. The men who make a law know what they mean by it, and therefore when, immediately after making it, they construe it by word or act, their construction is of high authority. Our constitution was construed, in respect of the special provision for amendment, immediately after its adoption, by the highest judicial tribunal of the State. It is well known that it was the habit of my father, the late

Chief Justice Durfee, to express his views on legal topics of general interest in his charges to the grand jury. He was a member of the convention that framed the present constitution, and its adoption would naturally suggest a charge relating to it. Until quite recently, however, I was unaware, or if I had ever been aware, I had forgotten that he had actually improved the occasion ; but a short while ago, in looking over his papers to find a manuscript pertaining to a different matter, I came across a charge to the grand jury, in his handwriting, indorsed : "1843, August Term, Newport." I see no reason to doubt that the charge was delivered at Newport, at the August term of the supreme court, in 1843. If so, it was doubtless delivered with the approval of his associates, one of whom was the late Chief Justice Staples. Again, if it was delivered at Newport, it was doubtless delivered, in accordance with his custom, in every other county of the State. Now a charge on such a subject, delivered throughout the State, must have provoked dissent and discussion, unless generally approved, and therefore the fact that there are no traces of any such dissent or discussion, shows that the doctrines proclaimed in it were then accepted by the people at large as indisputably correct. No document, therefore, could afford better proof of what was the prevalent construction of the constitution at the time of its adoption.

The charge begins with an exposition of the Anglo-American idea of political or constitutional sovereignty, tracing it back to its sources in English history and jurisprudence, following it in its evolution as it defines and purifies itself, explaining its operation under the old charter, before and after the Revolution, and finally setting forth the proceeding by which the State, without any interruption of its continuity, legally exchanged the charter for the constitution. The charge then, after indicating some of the more important changes introduced by the constitution, proceeded as follows, considering the question which has so long occupied our attention :

" With the exception of a few restrictions, the legislative power, by an express provision of the constitution, remains the same as under the charter. Among these restrictions, however, is one of great importance. It relates to the manner in which the constitution may be amended. When a constitution prescribes no particular mode of amendment, it is by no means to be inferred from that fact that it cannot be amended. On the contrary, the power of amendment is more ample than with a particular provision for that purpose. In such case, the organized people, acting through their legislature, may prescribe any mode that may be deemed most expedient, taking care not to violate those fundamental principles of individual right which lie at the foundations of all constitutional governments. But when a particular mode is pointed out in the constitution it must be pursued, for to disregard it is to act in violation of a constitutional provision which we are all, and particularly the sworn officers of the State, under the most solemn obligations to support. A change brought about by any other mode than that prescribed by the constitution, when such mode is prescribed by it, would be revolutionary. It was by a departure from the mode of amendment prescribed by the French constitution and by submitting the question directly to the people that Napoleon Bonaparte made himself consul for life, and afterwards emperor of France. This might be tolerated as constitutional law, or rather as an evil to be borne, in revolutionary France, but not in the Anglo-American States of this continent. Here we must be governed by the provisions of our constitutions. The sworn officers of the State must not incur the guilt of perjury by violating them, and we must all recollect, that when we wilfully and knowingly depart from them, there is no middle ground on which we can stop in our revolutionary progress, short of unmitigated absolute military despotism. Once establish it as constitutional law in this Union, that an article providing for the amendment of a constitution may be disregarded, or a change of government effected without pursuing a legal course, and the last trumpet has sounded and the day of doom has come to our political institutions. What could prevent some popular chief who happened to be President of the United States from treading in the footsteps of Napoleon to a throne? There are no limits to the madness of faction, and there is nothing too extravagant for masses of men under the influence of a temporary insanity to attempt and carry into effect."

I have now said all that I wish to say on this subject. I have met all of Judge Bradley's arguments. I have endeavored to express myself with plainness and simplicity. I am afraid that I may have been tedious in my desire to be intelligible; but if so, the motive must be my apology. I hope I have succeeded in making myself perfectly understood. If I have, I am content; for then I know that my readers can readily find whether I am right or wrong in my conclusions, and I shall cheerfully submit to their verdict.